For Ursula and Suki,
with love, Giles

For the Gerrard family.
You throw the best
Halloween party!
With love from Emma x

ORCHARD BOOKS

First published in Great Britain in 2019 by The Watts Publishing Group

1 3 5 7 9 10 8 6 4 2

Text © Giles Andreae 2019
Illustrations © Emma Dodd 2019

The moral rights of the author and illustrator have been asserted.

A CIP catalogue record for this book is available from the British Library.

ISBN 978 1 40833 968 8

Printed and bound in China

FSC
www.fsc.org

MIX
Paper from
responsible sources
FSC® C104740

Orchard Books
An imprint of Hachette Children's Group
Part of The Watts Publishing Group Limited
Carmelite House, 50 Victoria Embankment, London EC4Y 0DZ

An Hachette UK Company
www.hachette.co.uk
www.hachettechildrens.co.uk

I love halloween

Giles Andreae & Emma Dodd

ORCHARD

It's Halloween today –
woo-hoo!

There's so much

spooky stuff to do!

Here's the pumpkin that I chose.

We carve its mouth and eyes and nose.

My friend and I make witches' hats And cut out spiders, worms and bats.

We've baked some ghostly cookies. Yum!
With sugar icing –
oh, what fun!

It's nearly time to trick or treat.

My monster costume's really neat!

Now Mummy paints my face. It's great!

I look so scary – I can't wait!

At last, my friends arrive, and so . . .

. . . we all hold hands and off we go!

We knock on doors
all down the street
And shout together,
"Trick or treat?"

We scare the grown-ups

just enough . . .

To give us loads of

yummy stuff!

Then home we go
for broomstick races,

Eating sweets
and pulling faces.

Now it's time
to say goodnight.
I cuddle Mummy
warm and tight.

"Come," Daddy says, "it's time for bed, You scary little sleepy-head."

So softly up the stairs we creep . . .

'Cause even monsters need their sleep!